# Fran Makes the Team

by Jenny Jinks and Nigel Baines

W

FRANKLIN WATTS
LONDON•SYDNEY

# Fran Makes the Team

## Contents

# Chapter 1
# Talent Spotted

"Time to go," Fran's mum called out of the window.

Fran looked at her watch whilst keeping the football balanced perfectly on top of her foot. She had been so busy playing she had lost all track of time. If she didn't get a move on, she would be late for school.

She flicked the ball up into the air and kicked it. It flew straight into the back of the shed.

"Goal!" Fran cried. She ran around the garden as if she had just scored the winning goal in a world cup.

Fran ran inside, grabbed her school bag and rushed out of the door. For now, football would have to wait.

Later that day, Fran sat on the school field with her friends. They were all busy chatting, but Fran was distracted. She was watching the school football team, the Fizzlers. How she wished that she could be playing with them.

Suddenly, the ball flew straight at Fran. She jumped up and kicked it back towards the pitch. It sailed straight past all the players and swished into the back of the net. Ben, the team's star striker, stared at Fran in amazement.

Fran turned to her friends to celebrate, but they hadn't been watching. They had no idea that she had just scored the most amazing goal ever.

But Mr Andrews, the football coach, had been watching with interest.

"Fran!" Coach Andrews raced up to her. "I saw you on the field. You've got some skills," he said, looking impressed. "Have you ever thought about playing for the team?"

"I don't know," Fran said shyly. But inside her stomach did an excited flip. She had dreamt about playing for a team ever since she got her first football when she was five years old. But she had never told anybody. None of her friends liked football. And she had no idea if she was actually any good. She had only ever played by herself in her back garden.

"We would love to see you at training after school tomorrow," Coach Andrews said. "Think about it."

For the rest of the day, Fran thought about nothing

else. This could be the start of her dreams

coming true.

# Chapter 2
# Odd One Out

The next afternoon, Fran stood outside
the changing rooms in her football kit. She was
buzzing with excitement.

"Great. You came!" Coach Andrews said. "Everyone's
out on the field warming up. Come on."

Fran heard the team players muttering to each
other under their breath as she joined them on
the pitch.

"A quick warm up and then we'll have a match,"
Coach Andrews said.

Fran could feel the other boys watching her, so she decided to show them what she could do. She flicked the ball up onto her knees and bounced it from one knee to the other. Then she dropped it to the floor and booted it as hard as she could. It flew across the pitch and landed right in the back of the net. "Yes!" Fran shouted.

She expected the boys to look impressed, but they had gone back to their own warm-up. All except Ben, who seemed to be glaring in her direction. Perhaps the sun was in his eyes, Fran thought.

Coach Andrews divided the team in half for a match. "Everyone, let's make Fran feel welcome," he said. But nobody tried to make Fran feel welcome. She felt like she might as well be sat on the subs bench. The boys didn't let her near the ball once. She felt completely invisible.

"Don't worry, you'll get the hang of it," Coach Andrews told her after the match.

Fran wanted to tell him that it wasn't her fault, that the boys weren't giving her a chance. But what if it wasn't true? A good player should be able to get on the ball no matter what. Maybe she just wasn't good enough.

In the girls changing rooms, Fran could hear the boys talking next door.

"Why do we have to have her on our team?"

"I bet the coach only let her join because he feels sorry for her."

"If we keep pretending she's not there, she'll have to give up sooner or later."

"Lets hope it's sooner," one of the boys said, and they all laughed.

"Well if she thinks she's taking my striker position she's got another thing coming."

Fran knew that last voice. It was Ben. Fran slumped back against the wall. The team were deliberately not letting her join in. They were never going to give her a chance. She might as well give up now.

# Chapter 3
# Never Give Up!

That evening, over dinner, Fran told her mum what had happened.

"Don't give up," her mum told her.

"This is what you've always wanted."

"I don't want to give up, but what's the point if they won't even let me play? They don't think I'm good enough. I wish there was a girl's team I could join instead."

"Why don't you start your own then?" her mum suggested.

"That's a great idea!" Fran said. She was sure lots of her friends would want to join a girls team.

But nobody did want to join. Fran put posters all over the school. But not one person put their name on the sign-up sheet.

Fran pointed out one of the posters to one of her friends, Ella. "Have you seen this? It might be fun."

"Fun? Getting hot and sweaty and covered in mud? I don't think so," Ella said.

Fran sighed. She couldn't have a girls team with only one person on it. And she couldn't go back to the boys team knowing what they thought of her. Fran's dream of being in the Fizzlers was over.

FOOTBALL FOR GIRLS!
I'm starting a team!!
Sign up and let's show how good girls can be! ♥ Fran

# Chapter 4
# Dream to Win

"We missed you at practice yesterday,"
Coach Andrews told Fran a few days later.

"Sorry, I was busy," Fran lied. "In fact, I don't think
I will have time to join the Fizzlers after all."

Coach Andrews looked at her, disappointed.
"That's a shame. With you on our team,
the Fizzlers would really have had a shot at
winning the championship this year."

"You really think I'm good enough?" Fran asked.
"You didn't just put me in the team because you felt
sorry for me?"

"Feel sorry for you? Where would you get an idea like that? I haven't seen someone with your ball skills in a long time," Coach Andrews said. "It's a real shame you can't join us."

Fran's mind was reeling. None of it made sense. If she really was good then why didn't the boys want her on the team? Was it because she was a girl? Or were they feeling threatened? Either way she couldn't just give up now.

"Ok, I'll see you next practice," Fran told the coach. She just had to prove to the team that she deserved to be there. Then everything would be fine.

Fran was ready and waiting on the bench when the rest of the Fizzlers came out for their next training session.

"Not her again," she heard Ben mutter.
But she ignored the looks from all the boys.
She had to stay focussed.

"Exciting news," Coach Andrews said. "We have our first match tomorrow. We'll just do a short skills practice today ready for tomorrow's main event."

Fran felt butterflies in her stomach. She should be excited. But instead she was worried. She wasn't ready. She hadn't had a chance to get the boys to accept her yet. Her first match was tomorrow, and she had no idea if they would even let her play. This could be a complete disaster!

# Chapter 5
# The Big Day

The next afternoon, everyone waited nervously for the match to start, but Fran was the most nervous of them all. Finally, the whistle blew, and the match started.

Fran tried her hardest. She ran faster than anyone else on the pitch. But the Fizzlers still seemed determined to ignore her.

"Over here!" Fran shouted to Dean, but he pretended not to hear.

"Pass it!" Fran tried again as Ben got the ball. The defence swarmed around him, but he didn't pass it, and soon the other team had got possession.

Fran quickly made a clean tackle and won the ball back. But no sooner had she got the ball than it was tackled back off her. And not by one of the other team, but by Ben.

"Hey!" Fran cried. "We're on the same side!"

It was almost the end of the first half and nobody had scored. Both teams were playing terribly. The Fizzlers seemed to be spending more time playing against Fran than they did trying to win. If the other team hadn't been playing just as badly, the Fizzlers would have been losing miserably.

Then Fran saw Ben running down the pitch. He had the ball, but he was surrounded by defenders. There was no way he could score. Fran was in space. She had a clear shot at the goal.

"Over here!" Fran cried, waving.

But Ben didn't even look at her. Instead he took the shot himself. It went way too high. The ball flew above the crossbar and into the crowd just as the whistle blew for half-time.

Fran had to do something or they were going to be out of the championships before they had even begun.

"Don't you lot want to win?" Fran said as the boys sat with their water bottles. The boys shouted for her to go away, but Fran wasn't going anywhere.

"Look, I'm not trying to take anybody's place, or ruin anyone's chances. I just want to play football. So let's stop competing against each other and start trying to win!"

Fran walked off, her knees shaking. She had done all she could. The rest was up to them.

But when they started the second half, nothing had changed. Fran about to quit the team. Then she saw Ben making a run for the goal again. Fran sprinted down the pitch to join him. Two defenders moved in on Ben. He stopped. There was no way he would score from there, and he knew it. Fran ran forward.

"Over here!" she called.

Ben glanced over at her. Then at the goal.

"Come on!" Fran shouted. "I can do this!"

Ben had no one else he could pass to. So he curled the ball to Fran. She kicked the ball. Time seemed to slow down ...

Fran held her breath.

The keeper dived.

The ball curved.

It flew straight into the top corner of the net.

It was a goal!

Then the final whistle blew. The game was over. The Fizzlers had won!

Fran went to shake hands with the other team.

"You know we went easy on you, don't you. We could have won easily," one of the opposition team said. "Nobody will ever take your team seriously with you on it."

Fran's face flushed bright red.

"Fran could run rings round the lot of you. We're so proud to have her on our team."

Fran spun around. It was Ben! Fran smiled at him gratefully as the other team walked away looking rather sulky.

"Are you coming?" Dean called to Ben.
"We're going for ice creams to celebrate."

Fran's shoulders fell. They were going without her.
Just when she thought things were starting to get
better.

Ben turned back to Fran.
"Well, are you coming?" he asked, smiling.

Fran's face split into the widest grin. She raced
to catch up with Ben and the rest of the team.
Her team. Finally she felt like a Fizzler.

# Things to think about

1. What is the main theme of this story?
2. Why does Fran want to give up her dream of playing in the school team?
3. How does Fran's mum help?
4. What does Coach Andrews do and say to help Fran?
5. Why do you think the boys on the team find it hard to accept Fran? How does Fran change their mind?

# Write it yourself

This story examines the ideas of overcoming difficulty and following a dream. Choose a main character who overcomes a challenge to follow their dream. It could be based on a real person or made up. Plan your story before you begin to write it.

Start off with a story map:

• a beginning to introduce the characters and where and when your story is set (the setting);

• a problem which the main characters will need to fix in the story;

• an ending where the problems are resolved.

Get writing! Ensure you convey the character's feelings and emotions. Think about how you will convince someone not to give up – use persuasive language.

# Notes for parents and carers

## Independent reading

The aim of independent reading is to read this book with ease. This series is designed to provide an opportunity for your child to read for pleasure and enjoyment. These notes are written for you to help your child make the most of this book.

## About the book

Fran loves football and dreams of joining the school team, the Fizzlers. When Coach Andrews spots Fran's football skills, her asks her try out for the team. But even when Fran proves her skills, the boys just won't accept her. That is, until it's the day of the big match ... and Fran's goal wins the game!

## Before reading

Ask your child why they have selected this book. Look at the title and blurb together. What do they think it will be about? Do they think they will like it?

## During reading

Encourage your child to read independently. If they get stuck on a longer word, remind them that they can find syllable chunks that can be sounded out from left to right. They can also read on in the sentence and think about what would make sense.

## After reading

Support comprehension by talking about the story. What happened?
Then help your child think about the messages in the book that go beyond the story, using the questions on the page opposite. Give your child a chance to respond to the story, asking:
Did you enjoy the story and why? Who was your favourite character?
What was your favourite part? What did you expect to happen at the end?

Franklin Watts
First published in Great Britain in 2019
by The Watts Publishing Group

Series Editors: Jackie Hamley and Melanie Palmer
Series Advisors: Dr Sue Bodman and Glen Franklin
Series Designer: Peter Scoulding

A CIP catalogue record for this book is
available from the British Library.

ISBN 978 1 4451 6521 9 (hbk)
ISBN 978 1 4451 6522 6 (pbk)
ISBN 978 1 4451 6944 6 (library ebook)

Printed in China

Franklin Watts
An imprint of
Hachette Children's Group
Part of The Watts Publishing Group
Carmelite House
50 Victoria Embankment
London EC4Y 0DZ

An Hachette UK Company
www.hachette.co.uk

www.franklinwatts.co.uk